P9-EMR-799

Thunder Horse

Eve Bunting

Illustrations by Dennis Nolan

A NEAL PORTER BOOK

ROARING BROOK PRESS

NEW YORK

For Anna Eve Bunting with love
—E.B.
For Rod and Pow Wow
—D.N.

Text copyright © 2017 by Eve Bunting
Illustrations copyright © 2017 by Dennis Nolan
A Neal Porter Book
Published by Roaring Brook Press
Roaring Brook Press is a division of Holtzbrinck Publishing
Holdings Limited Partnership
175 Fifth Avenue, New York, New York 10010
The art for this book was created using colored pencils over watercolor washes on watercolor paper.
mackids.com

Library of Congress Cataloging-in-Publication Data

Names: Bunting, Eve, 1928– author. | Nolan, Dennis, 1945– illustrator.
Title: Thunder horse / Eve Bunting ; illustrated by Dennis Nolan.
Description: First edition. | New York : Roaring Brook Press, 2017. | "A Neal
    Porter Book." | Summary: Relates the friendship and love between a little
    girl and the winged horse she receives as a gift.
Identifiers: LCCN 2016058276 | ISBN 9781626724433 (hardcover)
Subjects: | CYAC: Horses—Fiction. | Magic—Fiction. | Friendship—Fiction.
Classification: LCC PZ7.B91527 Tj 2017 | DDC [E]—dc23
LC record available at https://lccn.loc.gov/2016058276

Our books may be purchased in bulk for promotional, educational, or business use. Please
contact your local bookseller or the Macmillan Corporate and Premium Sales Department
at (800) 221-7945 ext. 5442 or by e-mail at MacmillanSpecialMarkets@macmillan.com.

First edition 2017
Printed in China by Hung Hing Off-Set Printing Co., Heshan City, Guangdong Province
1 3 5 7 9 10 8 6 4 2

M y Aunt Aldora gave me a tiny horse, no bigger than a puppy. He was pure white and perfect in every way.

"Where did you get him?" I asked.

"On a hidden Greek island," she said. "I brought him home for you because I know how you like wondrous things."

She smoothed the mane of the tiny horse and he gave a soft whinny.

I stared, goofy-eyed.

"He's for me? Will he get bigger?"

"Yes. He will grow and change. And when he does he will want to leave. He's a magical creature and you cannot own magic. But he will feel your love and that will keep him with you for a while."

I looked into his eyes and whispered, "I love you already."

"What shall I call him?" I asked.

"Don't name him yet. His name will come to you," she said. As always, Aunt Aldora explained nothing.

She left the next day, as quietly as she'd come.

Dad shook his head. "She's like quicksilver. There's no way to keep hold of her."

My mother got a carrot and I grated it for my little horse. He ate from my hand and drank milk-water from a dish.

I let him lie in bed beside me. Sometimes he kicked his legs and made strange sounds, as if he were dreaming. Then I'd hold his little hoof, stroke him, and sing "Toora loora loora," the lullaby my mom used to sing to me.

One night, as I was petting him I discovered that he had tiny nubs on his shoulders. They might have been horns. But they weren't.

We bought a collar and leash for him and he and I went on walks.

People stopped to wonder at him.

By the
third week
I noticed that the
nubs were growing.

The hair on them was not smooth
but layered, like
beautiful white
feathers.

The week after, it was easy to see that my little
horse was growing wings.
"A winged horse!" My parents were astounded.
"I should have guessed," Dad said. "Trust
Aldora to bring you something so strange!"

I took my horse to school
for sharing. My teacher,
Miss Chalmers,
was agog.

"A winged horse!" She took a book of Greek myths from
her shelf. She sat on the edge of her desk and read us the
story of Pegasus, the winged thunder horse who lived in
the palace of the Greek god, Zeus.

"He became part of a beautiful constellation of stars,"
she said. "Look up in the night sky and you can see him."

That's when I knew what his name had to be.

Pegasus.

My Thunder Horse.

That night I tried to find him in the sky, but I couldn't
pick him out.

There weren't enough stars.

Pegasus ate oats and hay and horse vitamins, and apples and carrots, just like a regular horse. He loved the Greek yogurt Mom bought in Joe's market.

Soon, his wings were as long as my arms. Sometimes he moved them up and down, as if exercising them.

I worried that our apartment was becoming too small for him. At night now he slept beside my bed, not in it.

I couldn't walk him on the leash
anymore, but he trotted next to
me when we went to the empty lot
behind our building.

I watched as he ran round and round, snorting, flexing his long, graceful wings, and I was always happy and relieved when he came back to me. What my aunt had said worried me. He had grown and changed. Would he leave?

One day, as I waited for him to finish his last run, he knelt down in front of me and whinnied. He was inviting me to ride him.

My heart beat fast as I climbed on his back, and we soared above our building, above the corner gas station, above Joe's market, above my school. Wind whipped my hair. Birds flew close enough for me to touch. Clouds draped themselves around Pegasus's head. Riding him was like riding through a dream.

When we came back to earth I felt wrapped in magic.

Every day after that we went sky riding. My arms clung tight around his neck. My legs seemed to power along with him. But underneath, like a stomachache, was always the worry.

Then, one night, as we lay side-by-side on the grass, he did not invite me to ride. Instead he laid his cheek close to mine. He had never done that before and I knew. I knew the time had come. My chest hurt.

"It's all right," I whispered. "I understand. Thank you for staying with me so long."

He looked at me as if he were telling me something, then spread his wings, looked back once, and was gone.

I watched as he rose up, up, till he was only a snow speck in the sky. That's when I cried.

"I've never seen so bright a shooting star," my father said. "It must be a comet."

I stared as it streaked across the sky and wondered. Pegasus!

On that night, and on many others, when a special comet flashes through the dark of the sky, I lie in bed, waiting for the snorting outside my window. When I open it, he's there, all a-glimmer, shining and beautiful.

I climb on his back and we soar above the city. We chase
the stars. We cross the moon. We ride the shadows.
The nights are our secret.
My aunt had said my love would keep him for a while.
It did.
And maybe, just maybe, my love is what brings him back.